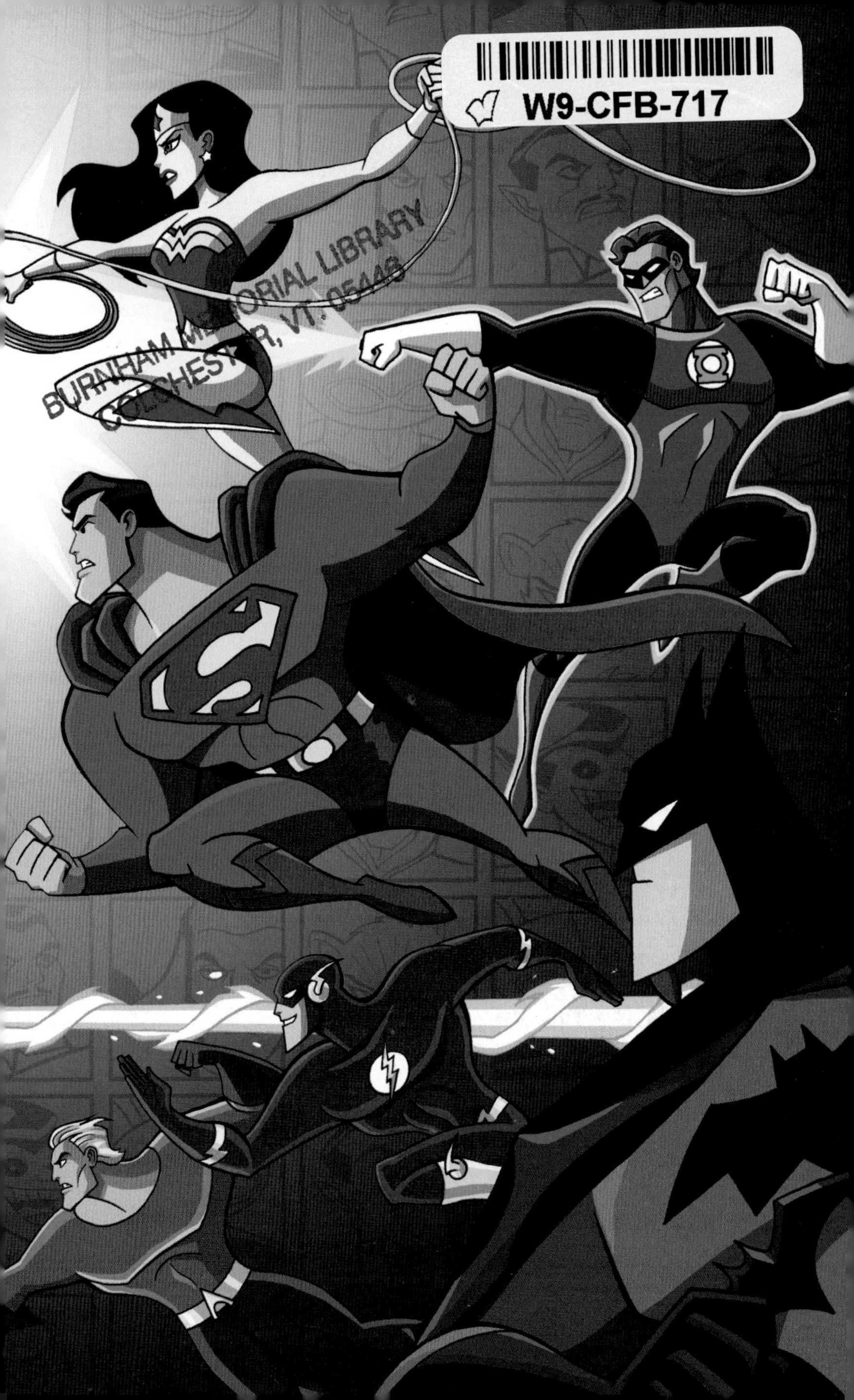

JOKER

ON THE
HIGH SEAS

WRITTEN BY
J.E. BRIGHT

ILLUSTRATED BY
SHAWN McMANUS

BATMAN CREATED BY
BOB KANE

STONE ARCH BOOKS
a capstone imprint

Published by Stone Arch Books in 2012
A Capstone Imprint
1710 Roe Crest Drive
North Mankato, MN 56003
www.capstonepub.com

Library of Congress Cataloging-in-Publication
Data is available at the Library of Congress
website.

ISBN: 978-1-4342-3794-1 (library binding)
ISBN: 978-1-4342-3895-5 (paperback)

Summary: When the Joker hijacks a ship in
Gotham Harbor, no one is safe. The self-
proclaimed Clown Prince of Pirates plans to
attack the city by boat! Luckily, two brave
and bold buccaneers, Batman and Robin, are
on the case. Will the Dynamic Duo swab the
deck with this seafaring super-villain, or will
they walk the Prince's plank?

Printed in the United States of America in Stevens Point,
Wisconsin.
102011
006404WZS12

TABLE OF CONTENTS

REAL NAME:
Unknown

OCCUPATION:
Professional Criminal

HEIGHT: 6' 5"

WEIGHT: 192 lbs.

EYES: Green

HAIR: Green

BIOGRAPHY:

The Clown Prince of Crime. The Harlequin of Hate. The Ace of Knaves. Batman's most dangerous enemy is known by many names, but he answers to no one. After falling into a vat of toxic waste, this once lowly criminal was transformed

Evil Genius

Bleached Skin

Permanent Grin

Joker Venom

Pain Resistance

POWERS/ABILITIES:
Possesses above-average strength; quickly masters new equipment; fueled by extreme rage.

CHAPTER 1

THE TOXIC DINGHY

Even though his arms ached, the Joker couldn't help but grin. The super-villain had been rowing for hours, but he was now less than a mile downriver from Gotham City. Besides, a little pain was nothing compared to the pleasure of finally defeating his archenemy, Batman. Tonight, there were going to be fireworks!

This plan is so perfect, the Joker thought. *In a short while, I'll make Batman disappear forever amidst a billion sparks of light.*

A sinister smile swept across the Joker's face. *Then no one will be able to stop me from plundering and pillaging all of Gotham,* he thought. *Just like a real pirate!*

Streaks of sunset appeared on the horizon as the Joker spotted his target. A giant cargo ship filled with valuable freight was heading toward Gotham. On its side, the ship's owner was printed in bold, black letters: WAYNE ENTERPRISES.

HAHAHAHA! The Joker let out a blood-curdling laugh and patted his inflatable dinghy. *They'll never see this coming.*

Joker steered his dinghy directly into the path of the *Wayne Wayfarer*. Then he slumped back in the inflatable boat, reclined his head, stuck out his tongue, and pretended to be unconscious. And then he waited.

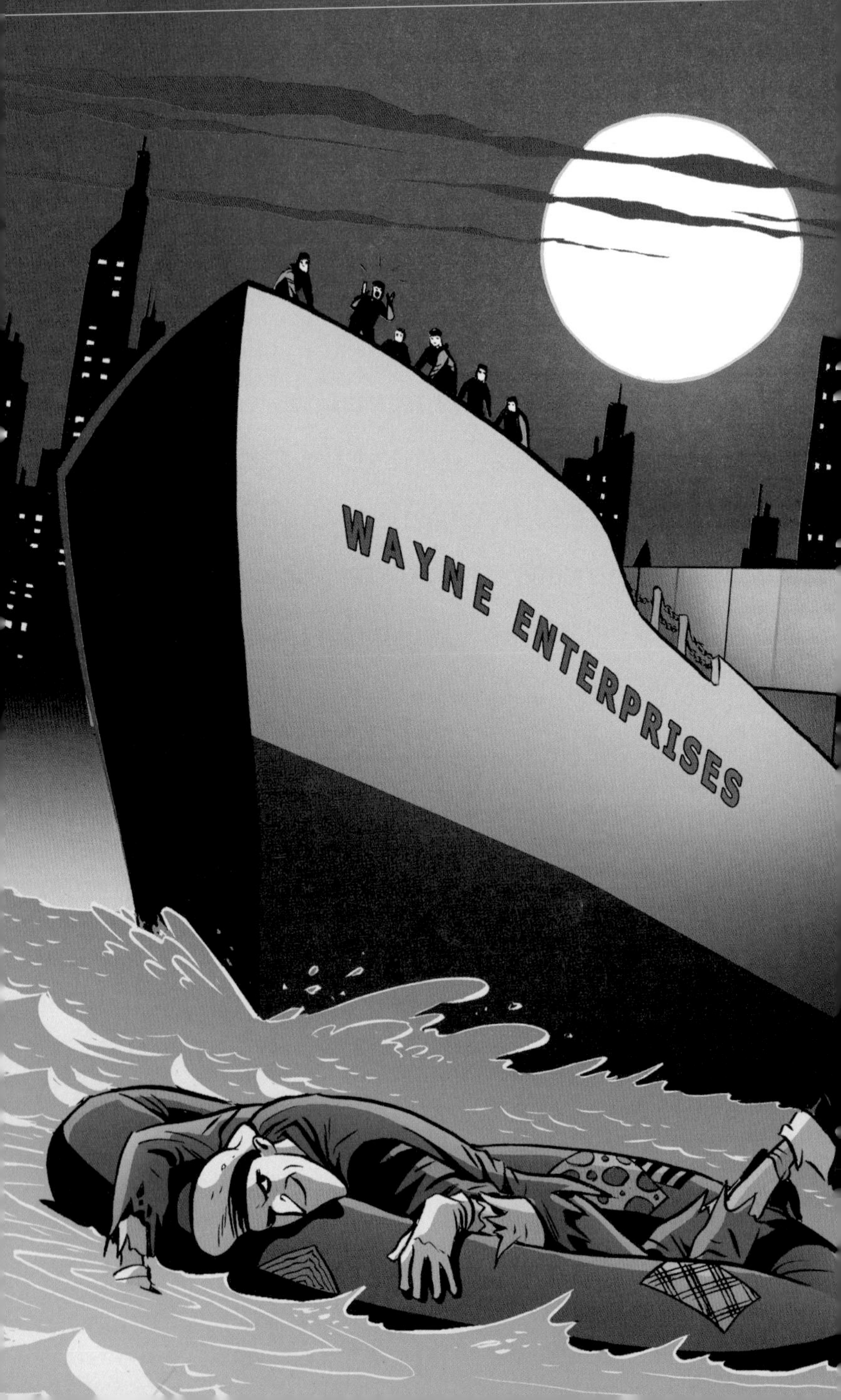
WAYNE ENTERPRISES

The Joker had disguised himself as a castaway. His purple suit was bleached by sun, and his sleeves and pant legs were in tatters. The Joker had covered his clown face with makeup that made him look badly sunburned. He even wore a wool cap to hide his startling green hair.

I must not grin or giggle, the Joker reminded himself. *I must not give away my true identity.*

After a few moments, the Joker heard shouts from the sailors onboard the cargo ship. The *Wayne Wayfarer* blew a warning horn, followed by more shouts and hails from the sailors.

The Joker remained motionless. He felt the dinghy lurch as it was hooked with a long pole from the deck. *I knew they couldn't resist a rescue,* he thought.

Soon after, the dinghy was hauled onboard the cargo ship. When it settled onto the deck, the Joker blinked his eyes and sat up. The crew erupted in cheers. All the sailors and deckhands were gathered around. Even the captain stood nearby. Nobody wanted to miss the rescue.

"Sir, are you okay?" one sailor asked the victim. "We don't have a doctor onboard, but we'll soon be in port —"

The Joker jumped to his feet. The sailors were surprised to see him move so fast. "Oh, I'm quite excellent," he replied, a wicked sneer crawling across his face. "In fact, I've never been happier!"

Then he pulled off his cap and wiped the makeup off his face. The sailors instantly recognized the super-villain. "The Joker!" the captain shouted.

The Joker picked up the corner of his inflatable dinghy. "Thank you for rescuing me," he said, "but who's going to rescue you?" He pressed a nozzle on the side of the dinghy, releasing a special toxic gas that had been inflating the little boat.

The Joker Venom gushed out in a thick green smoke. It billowed around the sailors, catching all of them in one big gust. The crew screamed and tried to run, but the nasty gas acted fast. Of course, the Joker was immune to his creation. But whoever else caught a whiff of it soon slumped to the deck, unable to move, with a eerie smile frozen on their face.

In seconds, the sailors were completely paralyzed.

"Now wasn't that fun!" the Joker said, dropping the deflated dinghy.

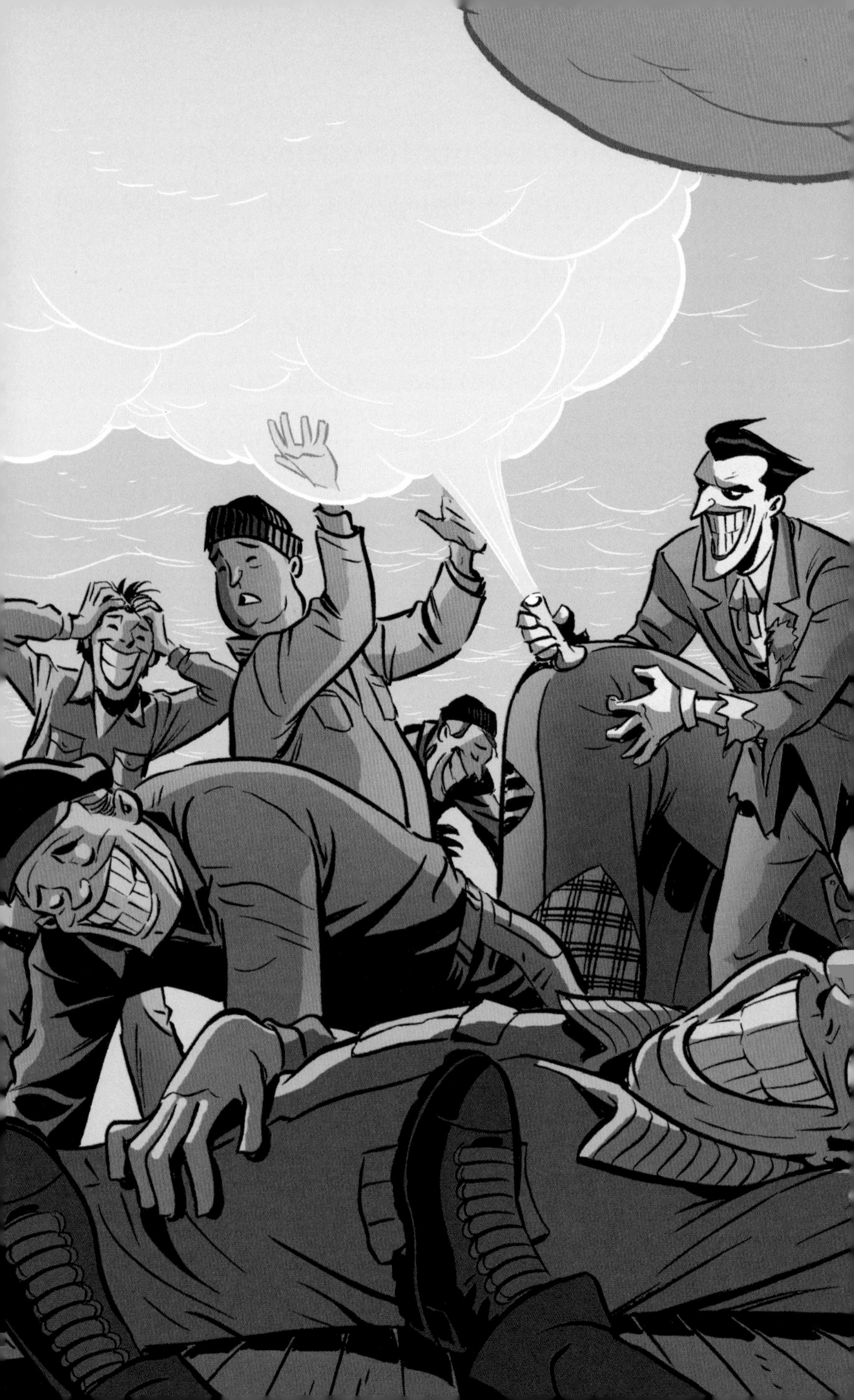

Joker strolled among the stupefied sailors, making sure they all were completely unconscious. "Phase One complete!" he said, clenching his fingers into a fist. "The ship is mine."

Standing on the bow of the ship, Joker gazed across the murky waters toward the Gotham skyline. "I've been this city's Clown Prince of Crime for too long," the villain proclaimed. Then he turned his head down river and looked at the distant horizon. "Maybe it's time to explore uncharted waters, and be crowned the Clown King of the High Seas!"

The ship is mine, the Joker repeated silently. He loved the sound of that. He glanced back toward the paralyzed sailors. *Alas, my crew won't be of much use,* he thought.

"Nevertheless, I feel just like a pirate," he said, cackling like a madman. He headed into the main cabin to take control of the bridge. A copilot was sitting at the main computer terminal. The Joker gassed him with a portable canister before the sailor even had time to react.

As he pulled the copilot's paralyzed body away from the terminal, the Joker noticed a ceremonial sword hanging above the huge windows on the bridge. "A cutlass!" he squealed. "That's the perfect pirate weapon."

The super-villain carefully ran a finger along its edge. It was as sharp as a razor. The Joker looked out toward the Gotham City skyline and grinned. "See you soon, Batman," he said.

CHAPTER 2

POLLY WANT A CRACKER?

As he strode across the ship, heading for the stairs to the cargo hold, the Joker peered at the parrot that was now on his right shoulder. But with the eye patch on, he couldn't see it. So he stopped for a second and shifted his eye patch to his left eye.

Now he could see the parrot. It wasn't a real parrot, though. It was actually a robotic creation with a built-in timer that he had brought with him. Joker giggled at Parrot. The robotic bird was the perfect accessory for the clown king of pirates.

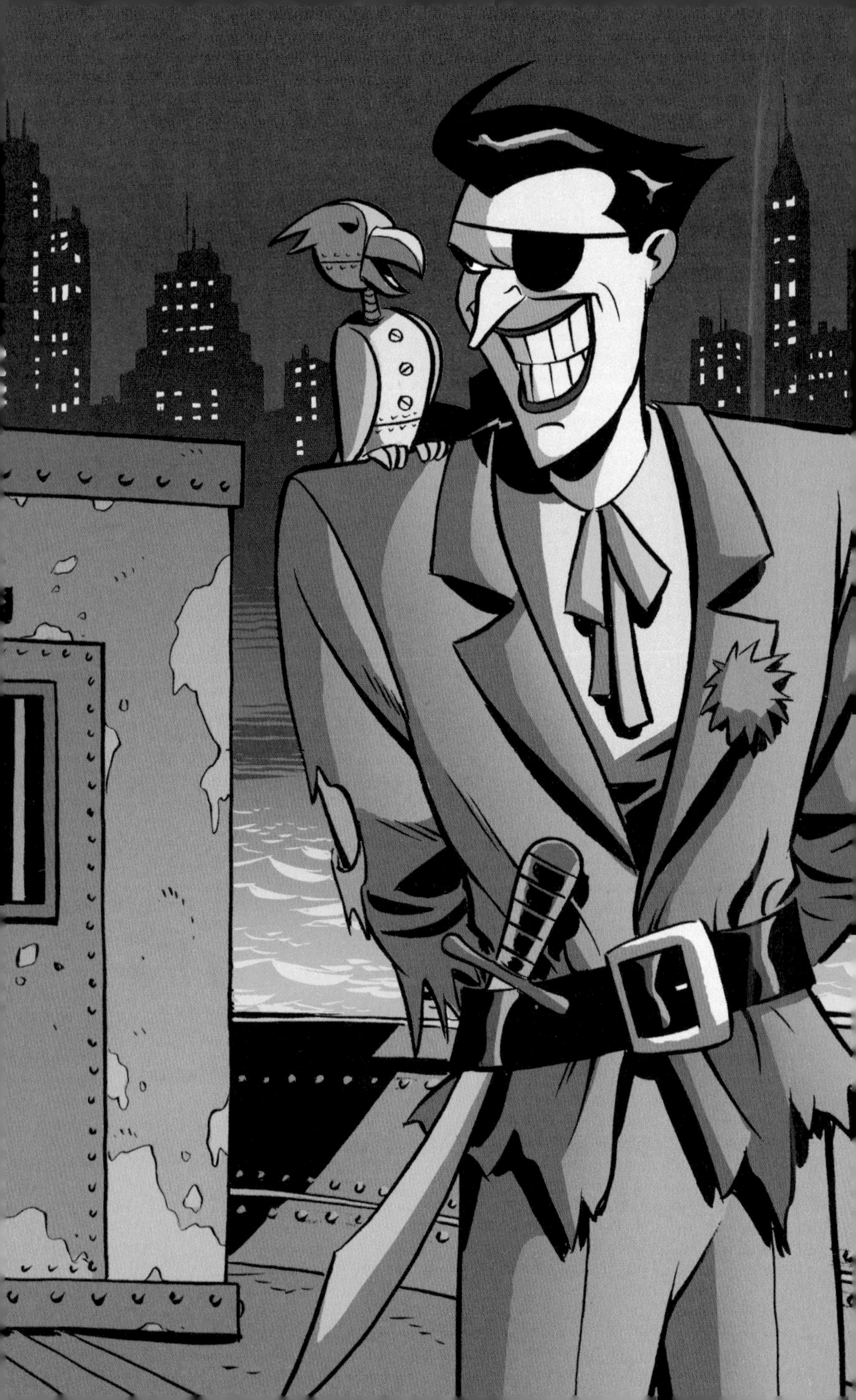

"Arrr, Parrot," the Joker said like a pirate, "want a cracker?"

Parrot glared at him with cold eyes and made a tinny, whistling noise.

"Aye, Parrot," the Joker said. "Sadly, I seem to be out of crackers. At least, the kind you eat, anyway."

The Joker chuckled and checked that his cutlass was still strapped to his waist. He looked every inch the pirate — a pirate crossed with a court jester. He smiled and hurried down the stairs to the cargo hold in the belly of the *Wayne Wayfarer*.

The giant hold was a transportation warehouse that took up most of the space inside the ship. The Joker turned on the lights and inspected the rows and rows of rectangular cargo containers that each held multiple tons of goods from overseas.

"My pirate treasure," the Joker told Parrot. "Arrr!"

The Joker strode between the rows, peering with his uncovered eye at the list of contents posted on each container. Most of the contents were pretty dull: refrigerators, super hero bed sheets, video game consoles, printer cartridges, light bulbs, and bookshelves. There was a whole row of containers holding nothing but paper plates.

The Joker stifled a yawn. "This is some poor treasure, eh, Parrot?" he asked, jiggling his shoulder to shake the bird's springy neck. It nodded in agreement and let out a mechanical *SQUAWK!*

Joker kept searching. Finally, near the back of the cargo hold, the Joker found what he was looking for.

There were three containers marked with the words CAUTION: EXPLOSIVE MATERIAL.

"Avast!" the Joker said. "I've found what I'm looking for, matey."

The containers were locked, so the Joker pulled out his cutlass. He sliced right through the plastic padlock on the lowest cargo box. Then he lifted the lid.

Inside were wooden crates marked DANGER: FIREWORKS.

HAHAHAHA! The Joker cackled. There were even more crates filled with explosives than he had hoped. He quickly got to work jimmying the crates open and discovered fireworks of all kinds.

Some of the fireworks were for personal use, like sparklers, firecrackers, M-80s, cherry bombs, Roman candles, and bottle rockets.

But those were all for child's play, and not what the Joker was really after.

"These are not the crackers we're looking for, Parrot," the Joker told his robotic bird.

In the topmost container, the pirate Joker found his true treasure. These were carefully packed crates filled with display fireworks — the type that were shot into the sky by professionals during July 4th celebrations. Authorized permits hung on the container wall beside the crates, which made the Joker giggle again. He was certainly not authorized to touch these fireworks, but that wasn't about to stop him.

This batch of fireworks, the Joker knew, was being shipped to arrive in time for the Gotham City Freedom Day celebration later that night.

The Joker had heard on the news that the fireworks were arriving a bit late, but that they would make it to the festival just in time.

Even better, though, was the fact that Batman would be arriving to investigate what had happened with the *Wayne Wayfarer*.

And the Joker would be ready for him — with brilliant explosives!

"I'll ruin Gotham's celebration by stealing their fireworks *and* destroying Batman in one fell swoop!" the Joker said gleefully. He turned to Parrot with a leer on his face and said, "How's that for getting two birds with one stone?" The mechanical bird let out a nervous squawk.

The Joker began carrying the fireworks upstairs to the deck.

The super-villain finished quickly, since he had planned exactly what he was going to do beforehand. By the time he was resting, the Bat-Signal was already flashing on the dark clouds above Gotham City.

The Joker cackled. Batman would arrive soon, and the Clown Prince of Pirates would welcome him with a **BANG!**

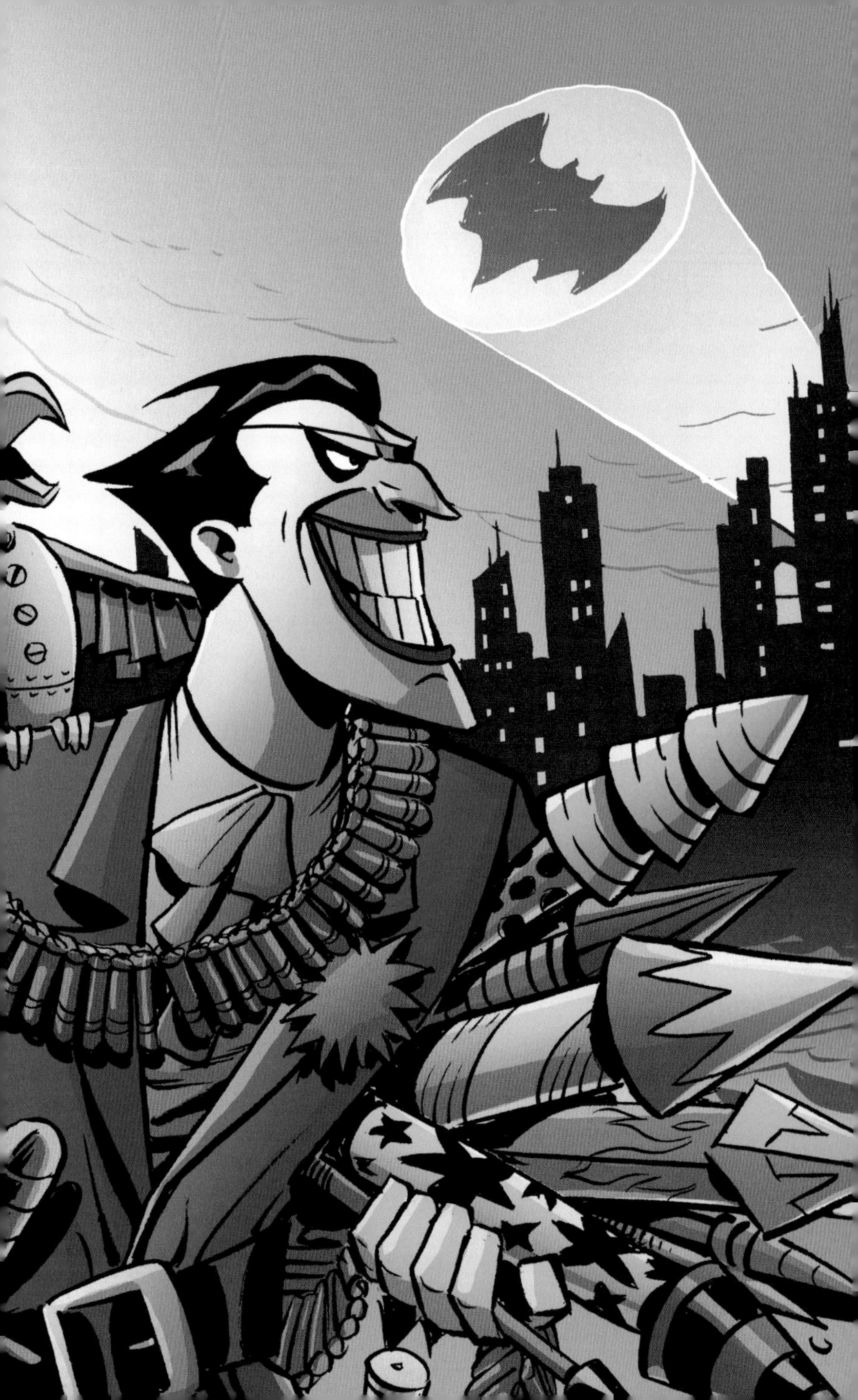

CHAPTER 3

FIRECRACKER ATTACK!

The Joker had just finished getting ready when he heard the Batboat roaring up alongside the cargo vessel. "Right on time," the super-villain whispered to Parrot. "Batman is always so punctual." Then he slipped out of the moonlight, hiding in the shadows of the darkened ship.

Only a single bell up on the bridge clanged softly in the breeze. Otherwise, the ship was eerily silent. The Joker crouched behind two barrels and waited. The trap he'd set for the Dynamic Duo was perfect.

The cutlass at his hip made squatting uncomfortable, but the Joker figured it would come in handy later.

"Hello, *Wayfarer*!" Batman hailed the ship. "Do you need assistance?"

The crew, of course, remained silent. It tickled the Joker to think how desperately the paralyzed sailors must have wanted to cry out for help.

"*Wayfarer*!" Batman called again. "You were expected in port hours ago! Please respond!"

After another long moment of silence, the Joker heard Robin say, "It's a Flying Dutchman, Batman — a ghost ship!"

"There's no such thing," Batman replied.

The Joker heard the clanks of two grappling hooks snagging onto the ship.

The sound of light footsteps followed, as Batman and Robin scaled the tall hull.

The Caped Crusaders leaped over the side and landed in a silvery pool of moonlight. The Joker watched as they scanned the ship, peering into the darkness.

Batman and Robin were right where the Joker wanted them. Trembling with excitement, he flicked a lighter, and ignited a long fuse by his feet.

Sparks snaked along the fuse, sizzling across the deck. The burning trail was too bright to go unnoticed in the darkness.

"Batman!" Robin cried. "Look out!"

Batman jumped to stomp on the lit fuse, but it was burning too fast to extinguish in time. The sparks reached their target.

BARROOOOOMM!

Thousands of small firecrackers exploded all around them. The air filled with gunpowder-scented smoke, lit up by the crackling blasts. Some of the firecrackers whistled and zipped around. Some emitted showers of multicolored sparks. Others popped with loud, flashing bangs throughout the ship.

Batman and Robin leaped, jumped, and dodged thousands of explosions.

Then the firework pinwheels and fountains went off. Hundreds of spirals of sparks whirled around the Dynamic Duo, blinding them with shimmering flickers. The fountains spewed out rainbow-colored sparks.

The ship's entire deck lit up, revealing the stunned, spookily grinning sailors sitting along the railings.

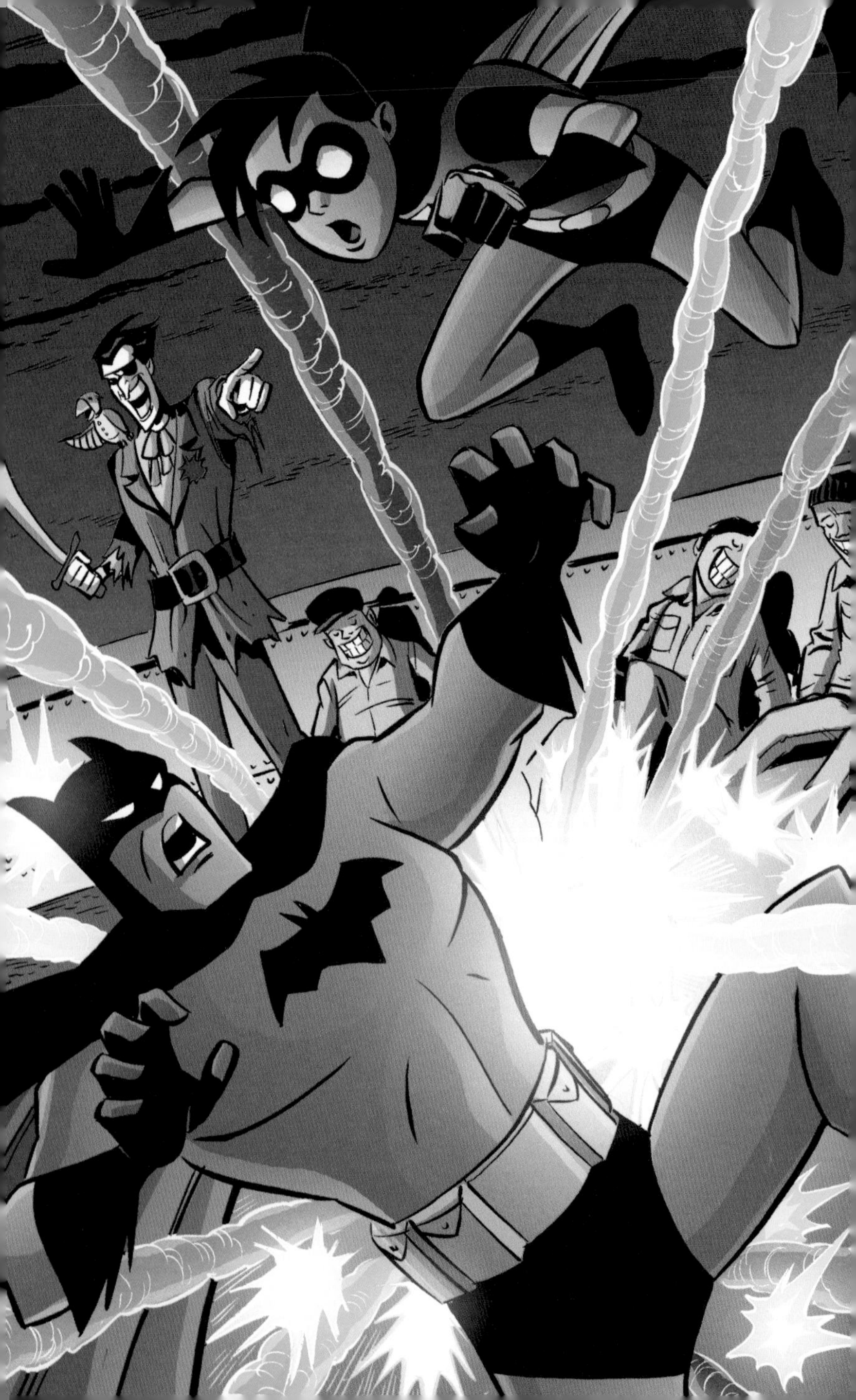

The Joker clapped his hands in delight. He laughed as Batman stumbled, dodging a zipping bottle rocket, and Robin cartwheeled to escape a Roman candle.

But the super-villain was deeply disappointed. With their athletic moves, the Dynamic Duo avoided any damage worse than a few singed spots. While they were still dazzled from the display, it was time for the Joker to make his next move.

He stood up behind the barrels, laughing loudly. "Did you enjoy my little show, mateys?" he screamed. "Arrr, you ain't seen nothing yet!"

"Joker!" growled Batman, spotting the super-villain through the firework smoke.

"Is that a bird on his shoulder?" Robin asked his partner.

"His name is Parrot, matey!" Joker replied. He kicked over one of the barrels in front of him. He had rigged it with an electronic charge that set off the gunpowder inside.

KA-BOOM! With a brilliant flash, a major firework blasted out the open end of the barrel. The sizzling missile slammed into Batman's chest, erupting in a plume of green sparks and knocking him backward. The Dark Knight tumbled down through the open hatch of a giant cargo container and hit the floorboards with a **THUD!**

The Joker kicked the other barrel over, but the second rocket missed its target. Robin leaped out of the way, rolling to the other side of the deck.

"Avast!" the Joker said. "One landlubber down."

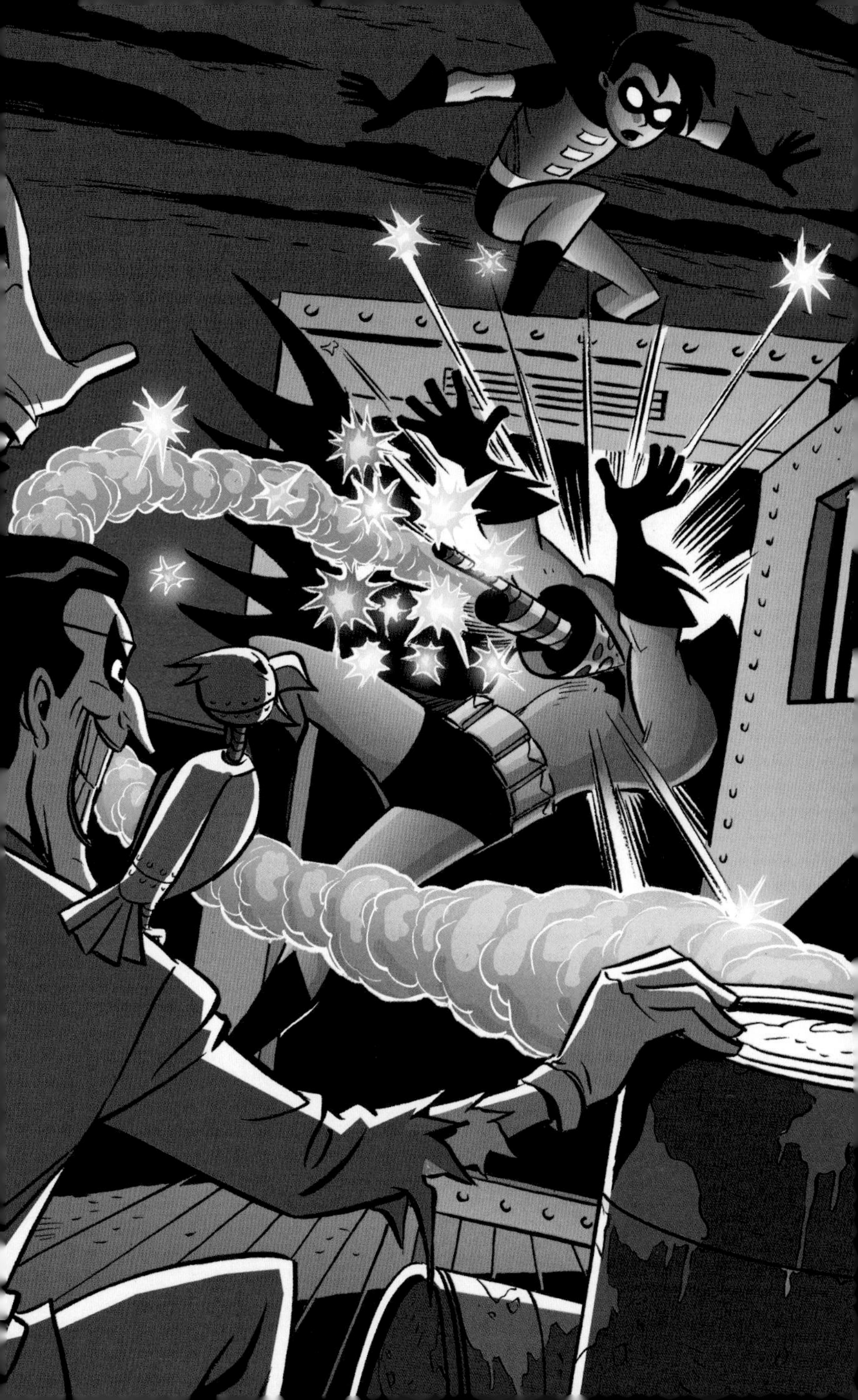

Joker sprinted over to the cargo container, slammed the hatch shut, and slid the bolt. Batman was trapped inside!

Then the Joker wheeled around, expecting Robin to make his move. He wasn't wrong — the Boy Wonder was charging right at him. The Joker sidestepped Robin's attack and grabbed a hanging rectangular control box.

With the press of a button, a crane swung its hoist, and snagged the back of Robin's uniform. The Joker pressed another button on the control box, and the hoist lifted Robin off the deck, dangling him helplessly in the air.

The Joker let out a shrill laugh. He had captured Batman and Robin. His explosive plan had worked perfectly.

Robin squirmed on the hook. "Let me down!" he shouted, kicking his legs wildly. The hoist had grabbed at the back of his uniform, where he couldn't reach.

"Not yet," the Joker replied. "We're going to have some fun first!"

"Now that I've got them trapped, Parrot," Joker said to the robot on his shoulder, "what should I do with them?" The parrot said nothing, but Joker leaned his ear closer to it. "What's that you say? Get rid of Robin first?" The Joker laughed wildly. "What a mighty fine idea, Parrot!"

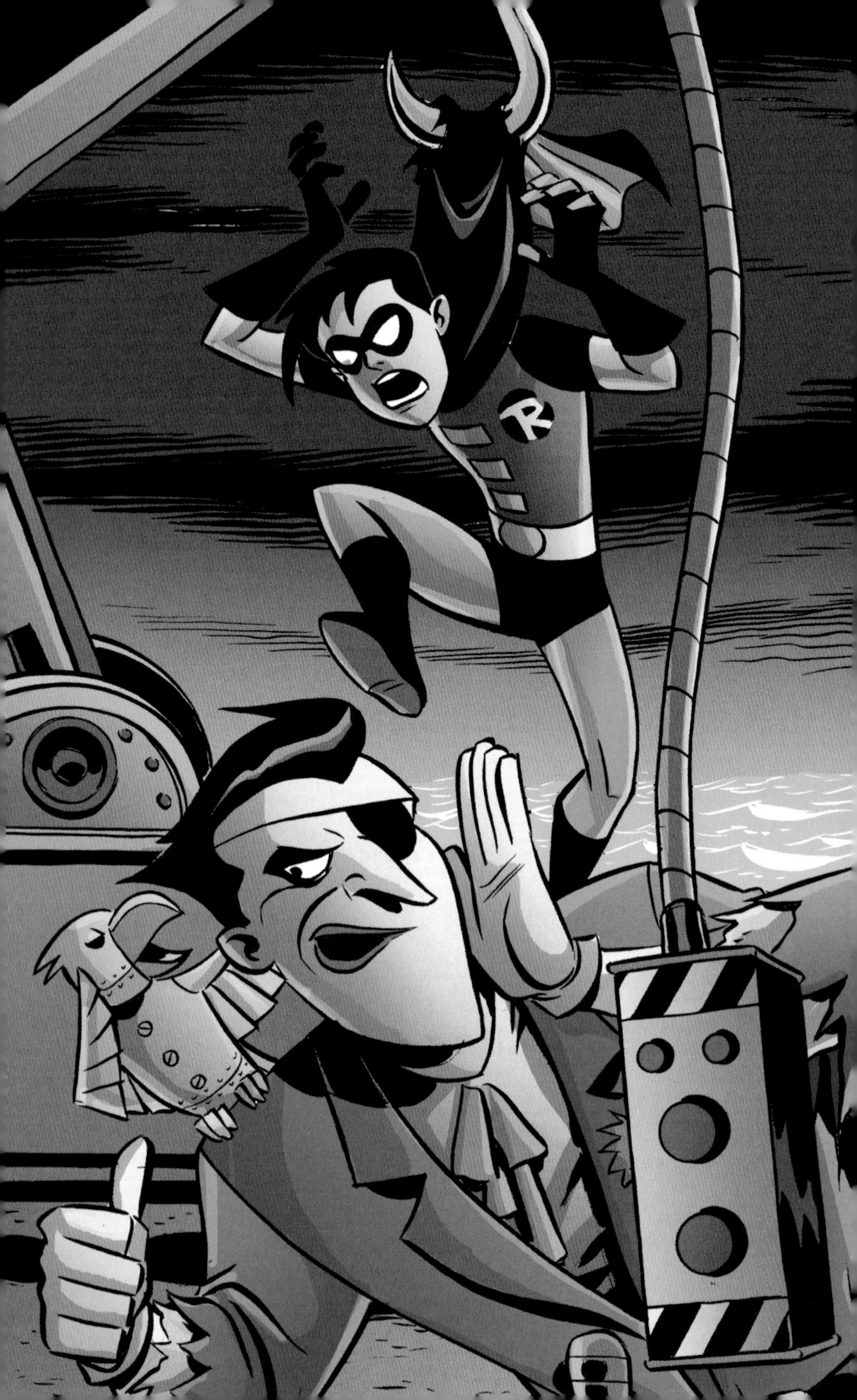

"You're crazy!" Robin yelled. "That's not a real parrot!"

The Joker ignored Robin. "And how should I do it?" he asked Parrot, cupping his hand around his ear. "Make him walk the plank?"

Parrot let out two sharp squawks.

Hmm, that's the parrot's timer, Joker realized. *Meaning my toxin will wear off soon. I have to hurry and dispose of the Dynamic Duo before the crew wakes up.*

The Joker lowered the Boy Wonder until his feet were just a few inches off the deck. Then he carefully looped a rope around them, keeping his distance. Robin could be quick — it was wise not to get too close.

"You're never going to get away with this!" Robin shouted.

"Hush," the Joker replied, pulling the rope tightly. Then he circled the young hero with the long rope, tying Robin's torso in snug knots. "There! Now walk the plank!"

"This is a cargo ship," Robin said. "You don't even have a gang plank!"

"Right you . . . arrr!" the Joker said. He found a long board and set it up alongside the railing, jutting out over the dark water. He shifted a heavy barrel to pin the plank to the deck. Then the Joker swiveled the hoist, and lowered Robin onto the board.

"I won't play your little pirate game, Joker," Robin said.

"Oh, yes, you will," the Joker said, growling angrily. The villain pulled out his cutlass and jabbed Robin in the back with it.

With the sharp sword poking him, Robin had no choice but to hop forward on the plank. "I'll get you for this, Joker!" Robin yelled.

"We all know robins can fly," the Joker replied, "but it's time to see if they can swim!" He thrust with his cutlass, and Robin toppled over the edge and tumbled into the water far below. There was a satisfying splash that made the villain smile. "Arrr," the Joker said to Parrot, "It's a pirate's life for me."

Maybe he should say something as a memorial for Robin? It seemed only proper. "Oh, Robin," the Joker began. "I never liked you. You were irritating. And I'm so glad you're gone forever. Farewell."

There! Now that was a fitting send-off for the Boy Wonder!

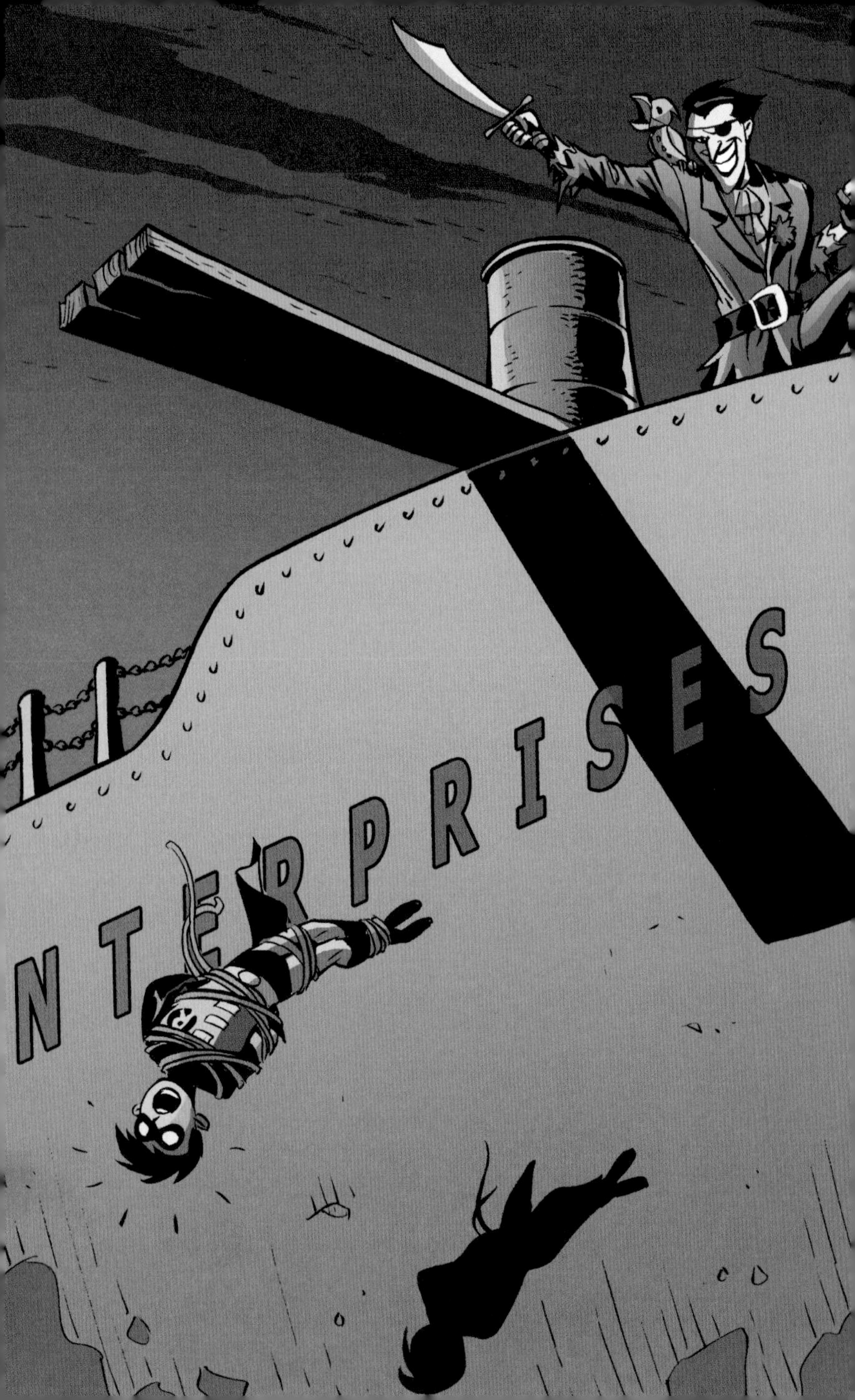
NTERPRISES

The Joker hurried over to the locked cargo container. "Batman!" he called down through the hatch. "I'm afraid your little Robin is sleeping with the fishes now!"

Batman didn't respond. The Joker squinted and stared through the bars of the hatch. He couldn't hear any movement inside.

"Did you hear me, Batman?" the Joker shouted. "Robin is fish food!"

Again, there was no reply from the Dark Knight. The cargo container was completely silent.

"He's gone!" the Joker shouted. "But that can't be!"

Annoyed, the Joker whipped out his cutlass. Then he slit the cargo container's bolt and lifted the hatch.

The Joker peered into the container.

It was dark, so the Joker lit a sparkler and tossed it inside.

In the flickering light, the Joker saw that the container was completely empty. Batman had flown the coop.

CHAPTER 5

GRAND FINALE

Just then, the Joker heard a sudden **WHOOOOSH!** He whirled around in time to see a dark shadow swooping toward him. Batman, swinging from a chain hanging from the crane rigging, slammed his boots into Joker's chest.

"Oof!" The Joker stumbled backward onto the deck. Then he instantly flipped over and scrambled away on all fours. "How —?" he gasped. "How did you escape?"

Batman landed in a crouch. "You forgot to close the ship's air vents," he growled.

"Sneaky Batman!" the Joker cried. He sprang to his feet and flashed the cutlass. "But now you must duel to the death with Captain Joker!"

"Captain Joker?" said Batman. "The only thing you'll be captain of is your cell back in Arkham Asylum!"

Batman kicked out, aiming for the Joker's legs. But the Joker jumped and swung down with his cutlass. His sword sliced through air as Batman shifted sideways, barely avoiding the blow.

"You'll never take me alive, matey!" the Joker cried. He ran forward, swinging the cutlass again and again at the Dark Knight.

Batman blocked a blow with his protective gloves then dodged a counterstrike.

The Joker knew he couldn't beat Batman in a fair fight on the deck. He had to reach higher ground. The super-villain faked another swing with the cutlass. When Batman prepared to block the blow again, the Joker turned around and ran. Then he jumped up on the ship's narrow railing. Now he had the height advantage.

With a swoop of his cape, Batman leaped and followed him. The Joker tried to slice him in midair, but Batman twisted acrobatically around the cutlass and landed squarely with both feet on the railing.

With an annoyed cry, the Joker swung his cutlass again, nearly striking one of Batman's pointy ears. He would have sliced it off if Batman hadn't ducked just in time.

"Give up, Joker!" Batman demanded.

"I haven't yet begun to fight!" Joker said.

Batman kicked up at the Joker's head. The Joker snapped his neck back, feeling the wind from the kick. Batman followed up with a fast punch, which the Joker blocked with the flat of his cutlass.

The parrot let out three quick mechanical squawks. That meant the crew would be waking up in mere minutes. He had to stop Batman now!

The Joker forced Batman to take a step backward with a vicious swipe of his sword. Then he leaped up onto a nearby cargo container. *Let's see Batman get up here without getting sliced up!* the Joker thought triumphantly.

Batman rushed over to the container, but the Joker's swinging sword kept him from getting too close.

Batman reached into his Utility Belt, pulled out a sharp Batarang, and hurled it.

FWOOOSHHHHHA! The Joker swiped the Batarang out of the air with his blade and laughed wildly. "You'll have to do better than that, Batman!" he hollered. "Otherwise, you'll walk the plank just like your stupid sidekick did!"

THUD! The Joker felt feet slamming hard into his back. He crashed onto the container on his stomach. His cutlass fell, skittering across the deck.

The Joker turned to see Robin drop from the chain onto the other side of the container. The Boy Wonder was soaked.

Of course! Batman fished him out of the water on the other side of the boat before he first attacked me! the Joker realized.

"Your little game is over, Joker," Robin hissed. "You're unarmed, and we've got you surrounded."

"I'm never done playing games," the Joker replied. "And I always have an ace up my sleeve." He rolled along the container, somersaulted to his feet, and leaped off the side — grabbing a chain in the air. The Joker swung from the chain and switched to the cable that held the hanging control panel. He grabbed the panel and pressed a button.

A huge crate of explosives lowered on the crane and dropped toward the deck. "I'll blow up the whole ship before I let you take me alive!" the Joker screamed.

The super-villain reached out with his lighter. Batman's eyes went wide, watching helplessly.

Just then, Parrot squawked four times into Joker's ear much louder than before. The noise echoed in the super-villain's ears, making his eardrums ache. The alarm meant the Joker Venom had now worn off.

The Joker rubbed his ear and knocked Parrot off his shoulder. It splashed into the Gotham River and disappeared. "Stupid bird," he grumbled. "Now, where were we . . . ?"

The Joker flicked the lighter, lighting the end of the explosives' fuse. However, the brief delay had given Batman just enough time to react. Swinging a fast crane winch toward the crate of explosives, the hero snagged it and swung it off the side of the boat. The crate hurtled through the air.

The explosives ignited — far over the water.

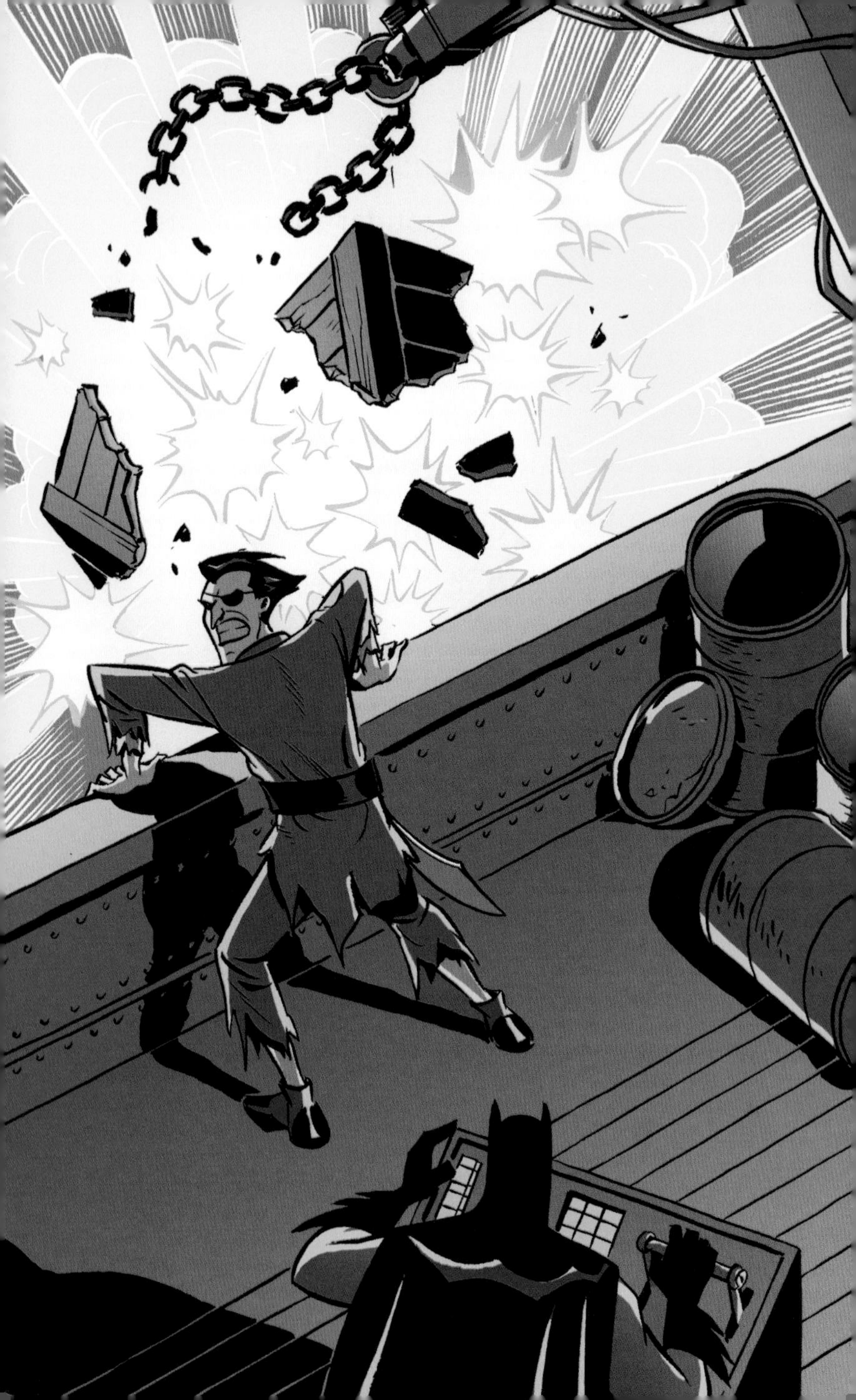

KA-BOOM! Hundreds of brilliant blasts of multicolored sparks filled the sky.

"No!" the Joker screeched.

Then he heard a horrible sound. People across the water at the Gotham docks were cheering the fireworks!

"Ooh!" they cried happily, applauding the firework show in the harbor. "Ahh!"

They had gotten their celebration after all, which made the Joker feel horribly ill.

Batman and Robin stepped closer, so the Joker ran to the railing — toward the side with the exploding fireworks — and threw himself into the air. He landed in the water with a splash.

The display of shimmering fireworks was still exploding above him, all the different cascades of sparks mixing together.

Lucky for the Joker, the fireworks would prevent Batman and Robin from following the direction of his escape.

The Joker quickly kicked away from the cargo ship. He found a wooden plank from the exploded crate floating in the water. He clung to it and caught his breath.

Unfortunately, he could still hear the cheers from shore. "Arr," he groaned softly. "Foiled by a flightless fowl."

But then the Joker giggled. "But you can't keep a pirate down. I will return . . . to have my sweet revenge."

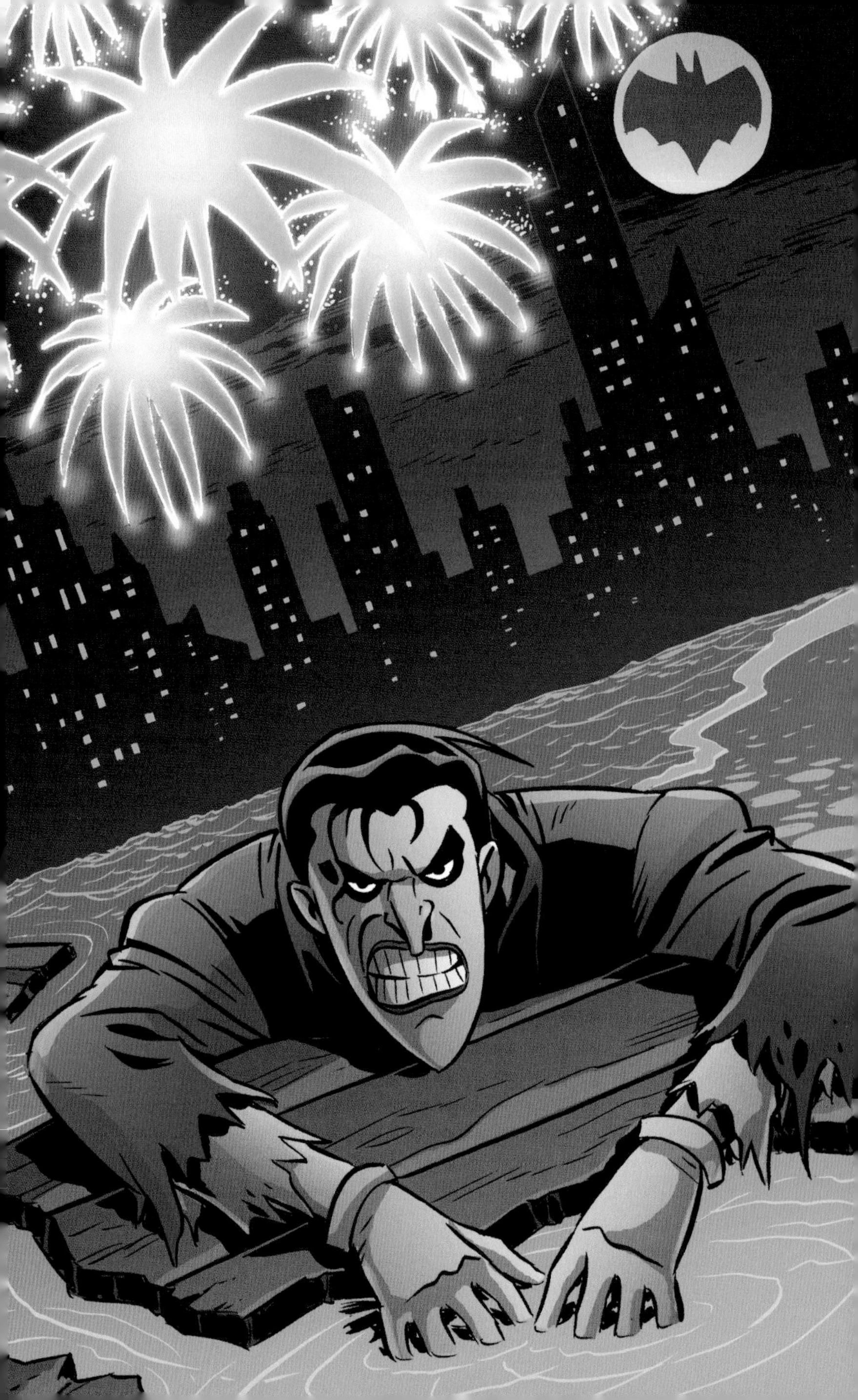

BIOGRAPHIES

J.E. Bright is the author of many novels, novelizations, non-fiction books, and novelty books for children and young adults. He lives in a sunny apartment in the Washington Heights neighborhood of Manhattan with his cats Mabel and Bernard.

Shawn McManus has been drawing pictures ever since he was able to hold a pencil in his tiny little hand. Since then, he has illustrated comic books including Sandman, Batman, Dr. Fate, Spider-Man, and many others. Shawn has also done work for film, animation, and online entertainment. He lives in New England, and he loves the spring season there.

Lee Loughridge has been working in comics for more than eighteen years. He currently lives in sunny California in a tent on the beach.

GLOSSARY

archenemy (AHRCH-EN-uh-me)—a major rival or greatest opponent

cutlass (KUHT-luhss)—a short, slightly curved sword formerly used by sailors or pirates

dinghy (DING-ee)—a small, open boat

hoist (HOIST)—a piece of equipment used for lifting heavy objects

hull (HUHL)—the frame or body of a boat or ship

leer (LEER)—a sly or evil grin

pillaging (PIL-ij-ing)—robbing and taking something away from someone else illegally

stupefied (STOO-puh-fyed)—stunned or overwhelmed

toxin (TOK-sin)—a poison produced by an organism

Joker Venom (VEN-uhm)—a type of poison the joker uses that paralyzes his victims and makes them smile like madmen until it wears off

DISCUSSION QUESTIONS

1. The Dynamic Duo manages to defeat the Joker. To even the odds, which villain should the Joker pair up with next time? Mr. Freeze? Poison Ivy? Someone else? Why?

2. Joker comes close to winning, but ultimately fails. Have you ever come close to succeeding only to fall short in the end? Talk about it.

3. This book has ten illustrations. Which one is your favorite? Why?

WRITING PROMPTS

1. The Joker's mechanical parrot is his partner in crime. Create a mechanical animal of your own. What species is it? What can your creature do? Write about your creature, then draw a picture of it.

2. What could Joker have done differently to change the book's outcome? What mistakes did he make? Write about it.

3. How will Joker get his sweet revenge? Write another chapter to this story explaining his next sinister plan.

LOOK FOR MORE

SUPER **DC** HEROES
-VILLAINS

LEX LUTHOR AND THE
KRYPTONITE CAVERNS

SINESTRO AND THE
RING OF FEAR

CHEETAH AND THE
PURRFECT CRIME

BLACK MANTA AND THE
OCTOPUS ARMY